Alec's
Primer

© 2004 by The Vermont Folklife Center

For information about permission to reproduce selections from this book, write to

PERMISSIONS
THE VERMONT FOLKLIFE CENTER
MASONIC HALL
3 COURT STREET, BOX 442
MIDDLEBURY, VERMONT 05753
www.vermontfolklifecenter.org

LIBRARY OF CONGRESS | CATALOGING-IN-PUBLICATION DATA

Walter, Mildred Pitts.
  Alec's primer / by Mildred Pitts Walter ; illustrated by Larry Johnson.— 1st ed.
    p. cm. — (Vermont Folklife Center children's book series)
  Summary: A young slave's journey to freedom begins when a plantation owner's granddaughter
teaches him how to read. Based on the childhood of Alec Turner (1845-1923) who escaped from
slavery by joining the Union Army during the Civil War and later became a landowner in Vermont.
  ISBN 0-916718-20-4
[1. Slavery—Fiction. 2. African Americans—Fiction. 3. Reading—Fiction.]
I. Johnson, Larry, 1949- ill. II. Title. III. Series.
  PZ7.W17125Al 200
  [E]-dc22

                                                        2003027716

ISBN   0-916718-20-4
Printed in Singapore

Distributed by University Press of New England (UPNE)
1 Court Street, Lebanon, New Hampshire 03766

First Edition

Book Designer: R. W. Kosturko
Series Editor: Anita Silvey

10 9 8 7 6 5 4 3 2 1

For Victoria Buffum
From family and friends

The Vermont Folklife Center Children's Book Series

Alec's Primer

By Mildred Pitts Walter

Illustrated by Larry Johnson

DISTRIBUTED BY UNIVERSITY PRESS OF NEW ENGLAND
HANOVER AND LONDON

NEAR THE RAPPAHANNOCK RIVER IN PORT ROYAL, Virginia, the Gouldin tobacco plantation spread over many acres. Each day five-year-old Alec went with his mama to the big house where he brought water and wood into the kitchen. Alec's mama sewed fancy dresses for Mistress Gouldin and her granddaughter, Josephine, who was three years older than Alec and called "Miss Zephie."

One day Alec ran into the sewing room. Mistress Gouldin and Miss Zephie were right behind him.

"Look at this!" Mistress Gouldin said to Alec's mama. She held a plate of cookies in the shape of soldiers. "Alec has bitten off all their heads."

Miss Zephie stood giggling. She loved seeing her grandma upset.

"It's not funny. He's an awful boy," Mistress said. "I want him out of the kitchen. Out! Take him to Presley. Now!"

Presley, the overseer, made sure all the slaves on the plantation worked hard.

"Oh, Alec," Mama cried. Big tears rolled down her cheeks.

"Now you will have to work hard in the hot sun."

"Don't cry, Mama, I don't want to be in that kitchen."

"Hush! We're slaves and work where we're told."

So before sunrise every morning Alec went to help
with chores around the plantation. He weeded and watered
the vegetables. He picked corn and dug potatoes. He fed
the chickens and gathered eggs. He chopped firewood. Alec
worked hard in the broiling sun. His clothes were often
soaked with sweat.

Sometimes he carried water to slaves working in the fields. Everyone wanted water at once. Presley shouted to Alec, "Hurry, boy."

When he was eight, Presley said, "You're a good worker. Can you behave if I send you to the milk house?"

The milk house! A cool place! "Yes, sir," he said.

Trees and a clear spring kept the milk house cool. Alec filled bottles for customers in Port Royal.

One day Miss Zephie rushed to the milk house. "I am sick of this place. Grandma gets on my nerves. I am going to run away."

Alec knew she was quick to say things she didn't really mean.

"Where will you go?"

"Up north to Vermont. Come with me. Up there, you'd be free."

Alec hurried to fill his bottles and went on his rounds. He thought about what Miss Zephie had said. He longed to be free, but he dared not talk about running away to her.

One day, Alec found Miss Zephie near the milk house reading.

"Come here, boy," she shouted. "Can you read?"

"No, Miss."

"Of course you can't; you're a slave."

Alec's face burned. He hated being a slave.

As she was leaving, she said, "I'll teach you."

That night Alec told his mama what Miss Zephie had said. "They put you in the field for eating cookies. For reading they'll sell you way down south. Miss Zephie knows we can't learn to read. That girl is trouble, Alec. Don't you do that foolish thing."

Another day, when Alec was loading the milk cart, Miss Zephie said, "Alec, if we go to Vermont, you'll need to know how to read."

Frightened, Alec said, "I want no trouble, Miss. I'm happy here," he lied.

"No slave is happy here."

Of course Alec wanted to be free. But could he trust Miss Zephie? He worked hard and kept his mouth shut. Sometimes customers gave him extra pennies. He put them in a jar. He hid the jar in their little cabin.

Miss Zephie came to the milk house often and read aloud. Alec listened and wondered what it would be like to read. Then one day Zephie came with a book she called a primer. "Alec, look at this book. Here, open it."

"No Miss, I can't."

"You must do what I say."

"I can't, Miss." Alec trembled.

"Take it!"

Alec could hardly breathe. He took the book.

"It won't bite you. Now open it," she said.

The markings on the page excited Alec. He wanted to know what they meant.

"That's the alphabet," Miss Zephie said. "A a, B b, C c. Now you say them."

"I must go," Alec said.

"Say them. When you say them all, then you can go."

While he was delivering milk, Alec said the alphabet over and over. That night he could hardly sleep. He was afraid, but he wanted to read so that he could be free.

Zephie told him that the letters had sounds. "We can put these letters together to make words," she said.

She gave him lessons reading stories. First he could read words, *"The. Man. Said."* Then sentences. *"The stars shine bright only at night."* "I can read!" Alec shouted. Now he might be free.

Miss Zephie just grinned.

Every day now, Miss Zephie gave Alec a lesson at the milk house. Then he went on his rounds remembering what he had read.

One day, Alec and Miss Zephie were outside by the milk house. Alec was reading the primer. Mistress Gouldin rode up and surprised them. "Zephie! What is going on?" she shouted. "You know it is against the law to teach slaves to read."

Alec was frightened. He jumped up holding on to the primer.

The mistress tried to take it out of his hand. His mind said to let go, but his hand held tight.

"Turn it loose!" she shouted, and slashed his face with her riding whip. Blood splattered all over. He looked her in the eye and held on.

Mistress Gouldin let go. "I will see that you're sent away from here," she said. Then she turned to Miss Zephie, "Get inside!"

Alec ran and buried the primer with his pennies.

"What happened to you?" his mama asked.

When he told her she cried, "Oh Alec, I warned you. They will surely sell you now." She washed away the blood and put a salve on the wound.

But nothing happened. Alec went on delivering milk and saving his pennies. He went on dreaming of Vermont and of being free.

In Port Royal Alec met other slaves who told him about men in blue coats fighting to free all slaves. Alec knew right away that he would like to join those men and fight for freedom.

When Alec told his mama that he wanted to join the fight, she said, "Alec, you're too young."

"I'm old enough to be free." He began to make plans to run away. Then one day he heard that the soldiers in blue coats were coming that next day to take slaves to fight.

Before dawn Alec went with others down to the shores of the Rappahannock River. Alec was afraid. He knew that if he were caught he could be badly beaten, even killed. Should he go back to the plantation? he wondered as they waited. And miss this chance to be free?

He stayed.

Finally, the soldiers came, and Alec was off to fight for his freedom.

Many years later, after the Civil War, Alec realized his
dream. He arrived in Vermont a free man, with twenty-five
dollars in pennies and the primer stained with his blood.

"Once you learn to read you will be forever free."—FREDERICK DOUGLASS

BASED ON REAL EVENTS, *Alec's Primer* recounts the childhood of Alec Turner (1845-1923). Born as a slave, Alec ran away from his plantation during the Civil War and joined the First New Jersey Cavalry in April of 1862. At first he served as an assistant cook—probably not cutting off the heads of soldier cookies. But, ultimately, he became an orderly to Ferdinand Dayton, assistant surgeon for the unit. During the war, Alec was wounded at Brandy Station, Virginia.

Dayton took Alec's continued schooling in hand after the war. While working in a store, Alec went to night school. Eventually, he traveled to Maine to find employment in the slate quarries in Williamsburg, Maine. In 1869 when Alec married Sally Early, the daughter of Jubal Early and his slave Rachel, they commissioned the wedding photograph on this page.

Many years after learning that he would be a free man if he went to Vermont, Alec met two men from Grafton, Vermont, who persuaded him to come work in the local lumber industry. So Alec and several other families, including Sally's brother, moved there in November of 1872. After several years Alec bought some of the land that he had cleared, about 100 acres, for a farm called "Journey's End." It was fittingly named by a man who had traveled a long and incredible journey—from a slave to a landholder. In this home he kept his blood-stained primer.

In 1888 Alec and Sally Turner had a daughter, one of thirteen children. They called her "Zebbie," in honor of Zephie, the young woman who had helped Alec at the beginning of the journey and taught him how to read.

Because of Alec's daughter Daisy (1883-1988), we know about his childhood. Through Daisy's many interviews with the Vermont Folklife Center, a rich collection of materials about the history of the Turner family—including photographs and audio and video recordings—has been amassed. Some of this information, including Daisy telling this story in her own words, can be found at (www.vermontfolklifecenter.org) the Center's web site. One of Daisy's own stories appears in *Daisy and the Doll* by Michael and Angela Shelf Medearis.

Alec Turner on his wedding day: 1869